Adapted from the screenplay by Ladybird Books Ltd.
Screenplay by Mark Burton, Bob Baker, Steve Box and Nick Park

Published by Ladybird Books Ltd
A Penguin Company
Penguin Books Ltd, 80 Strand, London, WC2R 0RL, England
Penguin Books Australia Ltd, Camberwell, Victoria, Australia
Penguin Group (NZ), cnr Airborne and Rosedale Roads, Albany,
Auckland 1310, New Zealand
All rights reserved

2 4 6 8 10 9 7 5 3 1

Ladybird and the device of a ladybird are trademarks
of Ladybird Books Ltd.

Manufactured in Italy

Wallace & Gromit™

Curse of the Were-Rabbit

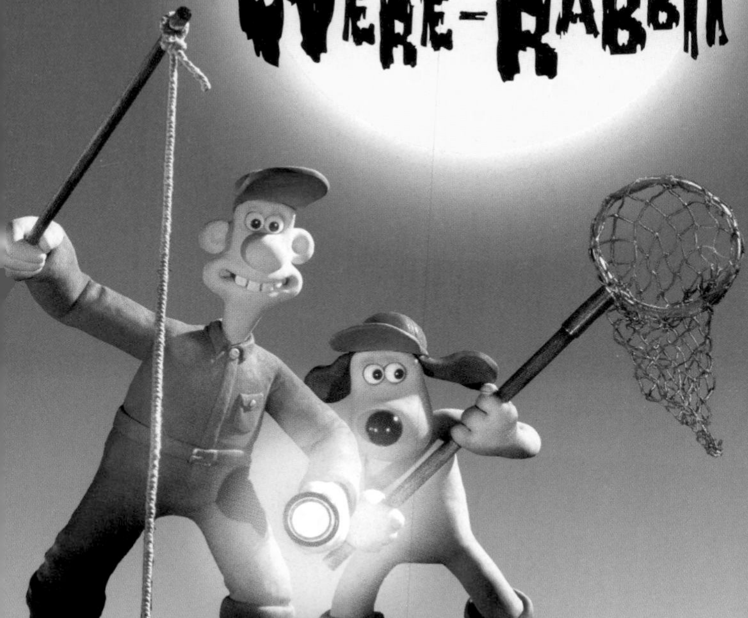

Ladybird

It was the dead of night in a sleepy Lancashire village. PC Mackintosh, on his midnight beat, was the only one still about. Or was he? The police constable had the uneasy feeling that somebody else – or something else – was watching him.

As a spooky long-eared shadow loomed over him, PC Mackintosh reached for his truncheon. But it was only the shadow of a moth, fluttering around a streetlamp.

'Albert Mackintosh,' sighed the weary bobby, 'you need an 'oliday. Too many late shifts – that's what it is!' And he headed off home.

But something was indeed on the prowl. Snuffling hungrily, the creature slunk through the garden gate of Mrs Mulch's house, paying no attention to the sign that read:

'PROTECTED BY ANTI-PESTO'.

Nor did it notice the garden gnome whose eyes began to blink red as it passed, heading for Mrs Mulch's vegetable patch…

In a nearby house in West Wallaby Street, a portrait of Mrs Mulch hung alongside pictures of other villagers. The eyeballs of Mrs Mulch's portrait were flashing. The garden gnome detector had triggered the alarm here in the headquarters of Anti-pesto.

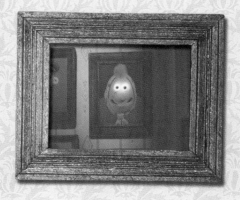

Anti-pesto was the latest brainwave of Wallace, a cheese-loving inventor, and his faithful four-legged friend Gromit. Together they had set up business as a humane pest-control team, committed to the protection of the local villagers' home-grown vegetables.

But now there was an intruder in one of their 'Valued Client's' plots, and the Anti-pesto launch sequence was underway.

A series of mechanical contraptions woke the sleeping pair, dressed them, gave them each a steaming cup of tea, and installed them in the front seats of their Anti-pesto van.

Within minutes of the alarm sounding, Wallace and Gromit were tearing along the moonlit streets towards the scene of the crime.

Arriving at Mrs Mulch's, Wallace and Gromit sprang expertly into action. With some slick teamwork, they'd soon bagged the intruder in a sack.

'Cracking job, Gromit!' Wallace congratulated his pest-catching partner.

The gigantic hulk that they'd caught turned out to mostly be Mrs Mulch's prize pumpkin, which a cute-looking rabbit was trying to drag off for supper.

The rumpus had woken the Mulchs, and their neighbours.

'Me pride and joy! You've saved it, Anti-pesto!' cried Mrs Mulch.

Her relief was only natural – the annual Giant Vegetable Competition was to be held the next weekend at Tottington Hall. Mrs Mulch was not the only villager who had her heart set on winning the coveted Golden Carrot Award for most impressive produce.

The onlooking crowd cheered Wallace and Gromit as they drove off, with the offending rabbit securely caged in the back of their van.

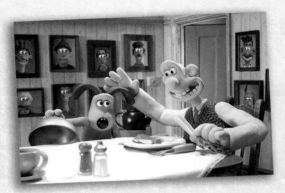

The next morning, Wallace woke up with a hearty appetite. He was disappointed when Gromit dished up a light, healthy, vegetable-only breakfast. Gromit was watching his master's waistline.

Overcome by cheese-cravings, Wallace tried to sneak something a bit cheesy from his secret stash. But Gromit had booby-trapped it, and Wallace was caught red-handed.

'I'm sorry Gromit!' said Wallace, remorseful.
'The fact is, I'm just crackers about cheese!'
Then Wallace had an idea. He could use
his latest ingenious invention – the Mind-
Manipulation-O-Matic – to extract all cheesy
thoughts or desires from his mind!

'It should be perfectly safe,' Wallace said,
fitting the contraption on his head. 'Just a
bit of harmless brain-alteration, that's all…'

But before he could try it out, a phone call
from Lady Tottington, of Tottington Hall,
in need of urgent rabbit-catching assistance,
sent him and Gromit dashing once more to
the Anti-pesto van.

The grounds of Tottington Hall, they soon
discovered, were overrun with rabbits.
'Only one thing for it, lad,' said Wallace.

Gromit nodded, and pressed a button on
the dashboard. The back of the van rapidly
transformed into a giant vacuum-cleaner-like
contraption – the Bun-Vac 6000.

Fixing its nozzle over a nearby rabbit-hole,
Gromit switched on the Bun-Vac.
Immediately, it began to suck rabbits along
their burrows, up the nozzle and into its
large glass collection chamber.

Elsewhere in the grounds, Lady Tottington was trying to stop her pompous would-be suitor, Victor Quartermaine, from shooting the unfortunate rabbits.

But Victor's plans were foiled when he found himself being sucked up by the Bun-Vac. Once freed, the humiliated Victor stormed off, unfortunately with a bunny on his head in place of his toupee.

Lady Tottington was delighted with Anti-pesto's humane pest control methods, and thanked Wallace warmly.

Back home, Wallace excitedly told Gromit that he'd solved the problem of what to do with all the rabbits they'd caught. They'd been looking after them in their cellar, but things were getting crowded.

Wallace's idea was to soak the rabbits in the Bun-Vac with his own anti-vegetable mind-waves, extracted using the Mind-Manipulation-o-Matic helmet. The brain-washed bunnies would then no longer crave vegetables, and could be released.

'Just a little added 'lunar power' to enhance the mind-waves,' said Wallace, setting up the equipment, 'and hey presto... Rabbit Rehabilitation!'

But when Wallace accidentally knocked the Bun-Vac lever to BLOW, the experiment went badly wrong. One little rabbit shot into Wallace's helmet, where its mind-waves merged with his.

'Oooh, eeeeeh! Get it off me, lad!' howled Wallace. Gromit acted quickly, smashing the helmet.

Despite the mishap, it seemed to have worked. The little rabbit – who Wallace named 'Hutch' – had gone off vegetables.

That evening, the Vicar, like other proud vegetable growers around the village, locked and alarmed his greenhouse. As he did so, a beast watched hungrily from the shadows.

The beast followed the Vicar into church, where it overpowered him and ravaged the vegetables on the harvest festival display. Then it rampaged through the villagers' gardens, devouring their beloved produce.

Wallace read the next morning's headline – 'NIGHT OF VEGETABLE CARNAGE!' – in dismay. The Anti-pesto launch device had failed. He and Gromit had slept through the entire calamity.

'Where were Anti-pesto when we needed 'em?' grumbled the angry villagers, at an emergency meeting in the church.

But when the Vicar told of his terrifying encounter with – The Were-rabbit!! – it soon became clear that this was no ordinary garden pest.

Victor Quartermaine, unimpressed, wanted to shoot the creature himself. But Lady Tottington insisted that Anti-pesto have another chance to catch it humanely.

As evening fell, Wallace and Gromit set out to trap the Were-rabbit, using Wallace's latest invention – a giant lady rabbit decoy, fixed to the top of the Anti-pesto van.

'Love, Gromit – that's the biggest trap of all!' explained Wallace, thinking fondly of Lady Tottington. 'And that's what we'll use to catch this thing!'

But as they drove through a low tunnel, the decoy was knocked clean off. Wallace walked back through the tunnel to retrieve it. As darkness fell, and the moon emerged, Gromit waited in the van.

Suddenly, the Were-rabbit appeared! Gromit tried desperately to alert Wallace by tooting the van's horn. When Wallace didn't show up, Gromit grabbed the controls himself, and set off after the beast.

Using one of the van's mechanical gadgets, Gromit managed to lasso the giant creature. But it was so strong, it simply pulled the van along, dragging it underground as it began to burrow.

The van hurtled along behind the beast, until the lasso snapped, and it quickly vanished into the distance.

Gromit, disappointed, drove steadily along the tunnel. Finally, as dawn broke, the van resurfaced – in Wallace and Gromit's own back garden! Giant rabbit tracks led from the burrow into the house.

As Gromit followed the tracks to the door of the cellar, he was quizzed by an annoyed Wallace, who'd been answering phone calls from angry Anti-pesto clients.

'Where did you get to lad?' asked Wallace, crossly. But as he followed Gromit down into the cellar, to where Hutch lay in the shattered remnants of his hutch, realisation suddenly dawned.

'Hutch is the beast!' said Wallace, horrified. 'The lunar panels must have over-stimulated his primitive bunny-nature! This is absolutely fantastic!' he went on, brightening. 'Okay, so we've created a veg-ravaging rabbit monster... but we've also managed to capture it, just like I promised Lady Tottington!'

While Wallace rushed off to tell her Ladyship the 'good news', Gromit began building an ultra-secure hutch for Hutch. Only when he'd finished did he notice something alarming – the giant rabbit tracks didn't, in fact, lead into the cellar, but continued past the door.

As Gromit followed the tracks upstairs, they changed from rabbit to human prints, leading right into Wallace's bedroom. Wallace, not Hutch, was the Were-rabbit!

Gromit raced to Tottington Hall, only to find that Lady Tottington was giving Wallace a private viewing of her rooftop conservatory, packed with luscious vegetables.

Gromit looked on helplessly as inside the glasshouse, her Ladyship showed Wallace ever-more-tempting vegetables, culminating in her prize specimen, an enormous carrot.

'Just imagine what it would taste like, Mr Wallace!' cooed Lady Tottington.

Sensing disaster, Gromit managed to turn on the conservatory water-sprinklers, bringing the romantic meeting to a sudden soggy end.

As Gromit drove his soaked master home, Wallace wrung out his tank-top crossly, puzzled why Gromit had drenched him.

Night was falling as they followed a road through the woods – only to find there was a diversion in the road, which led to a track blocked by a fallen tree.

Suddenly, Victor Quartermaine appeared, brandishing an axe. It was an ambush! Victor had witnessed Wallace's rooftop rendezvous with Lady Tottington, and was furious that Wallace was spoiling his chances of snaring her Ladyship – and her fortune!

'I've spent a long time reeling in that fluffy-headed bunny-lover!' he snarled, preparing to give Wallace a good hiding, as Philip growled threateningly at Gromit.

But then, as the moon appeared, Wallace transformed into the Were-rabbit! Flinging the fallen tree aside, the beast bounded off, leaving Victor and Philip scared and aghast.

Next morning, Wallace dropped into his breakfast seat, blissfully unaware of his monstrous secret – and the fact that he'd now sprouted furry rabbit ears!

Even when Gromit used a mirror to show him his peculiar new feature, Wallace refused to accept that he was the beast making the newspaper headlines.

'Silly old pooch!' he said. 'Next thing, you'll be saying Hutch is turning into me! Ha!' But when he saw that Hutch had indeed transformed into a rabbity version of him, Wallace finally accepted the terrible truth...

Meanwhile, following his encounter in the woods, Victor had paid a visit to the Vicar. The Vicar not only equipped him with three golden bullets – special ammunition for Were-rabbit hunters – but also warned Victor to take extra care and 'beware the beast within!'

Pressured by the villagers, Lady Tottington was forced to give him permission to shoot the beast, so that the Giant Vegetable Competition could go ahead.

Wallace spent the day desperately trying
to repair the smashed Mind-Manipulation-o-
Matic contraption, so that he could reverse
the ill-fated experiment. By the evening, he
was distraught.

'Oh, it's hopeless!' he said despairingly to
Gromit and Hutch. 'Me mind's just a rabbity-
mush. I'll never fix the flippin' thing...'

To make matters worse, the doorbell rang. It
was Lady Tottington, come to tell Wallace
that Victor was going to shoot the beast.

Concealing his rabbity ears in a hat, Wallace spoke to her on the doorstep. But with the fading light, he was beginning to transform again. As she tried to tell him that she had feelings for him, Wallace was forced to cut her off rudely.

'Feelings? Oh well, never mind, eh? Ta-ta then!'

As Lady Tottington headed home in tears, another caller arrived in West Wallaby Street. It was Victor, armed with shotgun and golden bullets, looking to shoot a Were-rabbit...

Gromit knew he had to get his master,
now fully transformed, out of harm's way.
He found the rabbit decoy that had been
knocked off the van, and climbed inside it.
Pretending to be a lovely giant lady rabbit,
he lured the Were-rabbit into the garden.

Grabbing a space-hopper, Gromit bounced
off across the neighbouring gardens, with
his master hopping eagerly after him.
And only just in the nick of time.

Victor burst into the house, and out into the
garden. Seeing the retreating beast, Victor
took aim with his shotgun, and let fly with
the first of his golden bullets.

In the nearby grounds of Tottington Hall
the villagers gathered for the Giant
Vegetable Competition heard a gunshot,
then an anguished howl of distress. Assuming
that Victor had succeeded in his terrible task,
and that their precious produce was now
safe from harm, they cheerfully got the
proceedings underway. Lady Tottington dried
her eyes and sadly declared the death of the
beast was 'for the best.'

But Victor had missed his mark. His shot had gone clean through the decoy rabbit's head, narrowly missing Gromit. The real Were-rabbit had made its getaway.

A furious Victor managed to shut Gromit inside a nearby Anti-pesto trap, then set off for Tottington Hall, where he was sure the vegetable-mad rabbit would be heading.

Thinking fast, Gromit cleverly managed to trigger a nearby Anti-pesto Gnome Alarm. He had to help Wallace!

Back inside Wallace's house, the now very Wallace-like Hutch suddenly found himself hurtling through the Anti-pesto launch sequence, ending up in the driver's seat of Wallace's van. Seizing the wheel, he tore out of the garage – through the wall!

The van smashed into the trap holding Gromit, freeing him. Gromit was about to drive off to Wallace's aid, when a plan flashed across his mind. A plan that involved the magnificent marrow he had been growing for the Competition...

Meanwhile, at Tottington Hall, the news was out that the Were-rabbit was still at large.

'Doomed! Doomed! Your vegetables are all doomed!' cried the Vicar.

The panicked crowd stampeded to the Competition Stand to rescue their produce. Attempting to restore order, Victor fired a shot – his second golden bullet – into the air. He told the frightened villagers that if they kept still, the beast would be drawn to the vegetables – right into his gun-sight.

But Mrs Mulch cracked. 'It's not gettin' my baby!' she cried, making a run for it, pushing her prize pumpkin in a pram.

Within moments the Were-rabbit was upon her, rising from underground to gobble the precious pumpkin. As it headed for the vegetable stand, which was heavily laden with produce, Victor expertly took aim. 'It's off to bunny heaven for you, Big-Ears!'

But at the very last moment, the Anti-pesto van screeched onto the scene. It was towing Gromit's giant marrow, with Gromit astride it like a cowboy. Luckily they managed to lure the beast out of the path of the bullet.

As Gromit's plan worked, and the beast followed the marrow away from danger, Victor, furious that his plan had failed, demanded more golden bullets from the Vicar. He refused, arguing that, 'they don't come cheap you know!'

Desperate for more golden ammunition, Victor wrestled the Golden Carrot Award from a reluctant Lady Tottington, and loaded it into a blunderbuss.

Hearing Lady Tottington's sobs of distress, the Were-rabbit rushed to her Ladyship's aid. He walloped Victor with a huge paw and knocked him into the candyfloss machine.

Clutching the terrified Lady Tottington, the beast fled from the advancing villagers, now armed with tools and torches. It clambered to the safety of Lady Tottington's rooftop conservatory, still holding her tightly, with Victor in hot pursuit.

Up in the conservatory, Lady Tottington feared for her beloved vegetables. But when the Were-rabbit put her down gently, and gave her a little Wallace-style wave, she realised its true identity. 'Wallace?'

Gromit, meanwhile, was doing his utmost to come to his master's aid. He had hotwired a fair-ride aeroplane to fly to the rescue. But Victor's rotten mutt Philip had hi-jacked another plane, and the two of them were locked in a desperate aerial 'dogfight'.

By now Victor had reached the conservatory. As he tried to brush aside Lady Tottington to get a shot at the beast, a slip of the tongue revealed that he too knew who it really was.

Lady Tottington was horrified. 'You're the real monster around here!' she cried. But there was little she could do as Victor cornered the giant rabbit on the rooftop, took aim with his blunderbuss, and fired.

In a last-ditch attempt to save his master, Gromit flung his plane into the path of the speeding Golden Carrot bullet. As the damaged plane plummeted to earth, the Were-rabbit leapt bravely from the roof and caught Gromit, and cushioned his fall.

A mighty whack on the head from Lady Tottington, with her huge prize carrot, sent Victor tumbling after Gromit and his master. He plummeted right through the roof of the Cheese Tent below, where Hutch had 'parked' the Anti-pesto van.

Hearing the angry mob approaching outside, Gromit quickly grabbed the giant lady rabbit costume from the van, shoved Victor inside it, and pushed him out into the open. The mob, seeing what they thought was the hated beast, chased the unfortunate aristocrat away into the woods.

Inside the tent, the Were-rabbit lay motionless, slowly transforming back into the recognisable shape of Wallace. As Gromit wept over his master's body, a last hope came to him. He grabbed a piece of nearby cheese and wafted it under Wallace's nose. It worked!

'Well done old pal,' said the revived Wallace, hugging his four-legged friend. 'We did it!'

Wallace's revival wasn't the only good news. Gromit was delighted when Lady Tottington presented him with the Golden Carrot Award – now a little battered – for his magnificent marrow.

And Lady Tottington? Well, she was very grateful to Wallace for saving her from a bad marriage, but a little worried that she would be rather lonely at Tottington Hall. As he prepared to head home, she spoke coyly to him. 'Wallace, I have a little proposal...'

A few days later, the friends were back at the Hall for the big event – the opening of the Tottington Hall Bunny Sanctuary! As Gromit used the Bun-Vac to blow their former rabbit inmates into the Hall grounds, Lady Tottington urged Wallace to come and visit sometimes.

'Oh – there'll always be a part of me here at Tottington Hall…' replied Wallace, warmly.

And as Gromit whacked the Bun-Vac onto full power, shooting Hutch into the grounds of the sanctuary, it was clear that he was absolutely right…

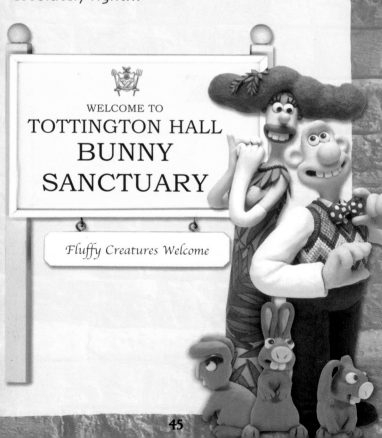

WELCOME TO
TOTTINGTON HALL
BUNNY
SANCTUARY

Fluffy Creatures Welcome